O'BRIEN flyers

Can YOU spot the kleptomobile
hidden in the story?

For Susan and Emma; Mad Grandad wouldn't be the same without them.

Oisín McGann began writing and illustrating stories when he was about six years old. His teachers were very happy about it ... until they discovered that was *all* he wanted to do. When he finished learning all the other things he had to do in school, he went to art college. They were very happy to let him go on making things up ... until they discovered that was *all* he wanted to do. After college, he had lots of jobs, but kept running into the same problem – people were always making him do other things.

Now he writes and illustrates books for a living ... because it was *all* he ever wanted to do.

Oisín has made up more stuff about Lenny and his Grandad in **Mad Grandad's Robot Garden**, **Mad Grandad's Flying Saucer** , **Mad Grandad and the Mutant River** and **Mad Grandad's Wicked Pictures**.

Mad Grandad
AND THE KLEPTOES

Oisín McGann

THE O'BRIEN PRESS
DUBLIN

First published 2005 by The O'Brien Press Ltd,
12 Terenure Road East, Rathgar, Dublin 6, Ireland.
Tel: +353 1 4923333; Fax: +353 1 4922777
E-mail: books@obrien.ie
Website: www.obrien.ie
Reprinted 2007, 2012.

ISBN: 978-0-86278-938-1

British Library Cataloguing-in-Publication Data
McGann, Oisin
Mad Grandad and the Kleptoes
1.Lost articles - Juvenile fiction
2.Grandfathers - Juvenile fiction 3.Children's Stories
I.Title
823.9'2[J]

3 4 5 6 7 8 9 10 11
12 13 14 15 16

The O'Brien Press receives
assistance from

Layout and design: The O'Brien Press Ltd.
Illustrations: Oisín McGann
Printed by Bercker in Germany

PEFC
PEFC/04-31-1478

CHAPTER 1

The Missing Clock

It was Saturday morning, and I couldn't get into Grandad's house. There was no **answer** when I knocked.

I looked in the window. Grandad was fast **asleep** in his armchair.

He didn't hear me knocking, so I had to get in through the **dog-flap**. The dog had died years ago, but Grandad had forgotten to get rid of the flap. I trotted into the sitting-room and woke him up.

'Grandad!' I said. 'I was knocking for **ages**!'

'Sorry, lad,' he blinked, and patted me on the head. 'I set my clock to go off before you got here, but it seems to have gone missing again.'

Now, Grandad was a bit mad. He sometimes heard music in the chimney, or thought the television was **watching** him. And whenever he couldn't wake up in time, he always said his alarm clock had gone missing. He even kept spare clocks in a locked cupboard.

He took another clock out and wound it up. Then he got me some orange juice and biscuits from the kitchen.

I went to turn on the telly.

'Where's the **remote control**, Grandad?' I asked.

'Oh, it's around somewhere, Lenny,' he said. 'Look under the cushions.'

I couldn't find the control, so I started reading my book instead. Grandad was nodding off in his armchair, so he set his **alarm clock** to wake him in an hour and put it beside him.

CHAPTER 2

They Came from the Sofa

It was very quiet until Grandad started snoring. And then something really **weird** happened.

A small, thin **hand** reached out
from under the cushions of the sofa
and turned off the alarm on the clock.

I crept around behind Grandad's armchair and peered out. The arm disappeared back under the cushions, and there was the sound of **whispering**, like two people arguing quietly.

Then a small **head** slid out from the back of the sofa and looked around. A little, bony creature climbed out and jumped down to the floor. Another one popped out behind it.

They were thin, lumpy and yellowy-grey, with two arms, **four** legs, and feet like **hands**. They had beady eyes and crooked little teeth. They wore lots of chunky jewellery.

Each little creature pulled a sock with **eyeholes** down over their heads and they started creeping around and picking things up. The taller one took Grandad's keys, and my book, but when the short one grabbed Grandad's glasses, I couldn't stay quiet any longer.

'Grandad! Wake up!' I yelled as loud as I could.

Grandad gave a yell as his eyes opened to find a little **monster** standing in front of him.

'We've got a **waker**!' the taller one shrieked. 'Every Klepto for himself!'

He leapt back over to the sofa, disappearing down the back of it. The short one screeched and darted after him.

I **dived** after the two creatures, and just missed the second one. But I was going so fast when I hit the sofa, I went right in behind the cushions and fell down the back of the sofa.

It was much **bigger** down there than sofas are supposed to be.

CHAPTER 3

Loads of Lost Stuff

I got to my feet and looked around.
The place was **huge**, and it was
packed with all sorts of stuff. Tunnels
led off on every side.

I heard a sliding sound and a thump, and Grandad landed behind me.

'Holy smoke!' he said when he saw the huge space down the back of his sofa.

'There's your **remote control**, Grandad,' I said, pointing at the remote, which sat on a pile of junk.

'You're right, Lenny!' he gasped.
'And there's all my old **alarm clocks**.
And my old army boots. And look!
Some of my pairs of glasses. I've lost
lots of these over the years.'

'You didn't lose them,' I shook my head. 'Those **Kleptoes** stole them.'

Just as I spoke, we heard a twanging sound. The two Kleptoes were making their escape by swinging like monkeys along rows of **springs** hanging from the ceiling. Grandad grabbed one of his old boots, and threw it as hard as he could.

It knocked the taller Klepto to the floor.

I sprinted over and jumped on him. The Klepto started screaming and crying and I got off him, but held onto his arm. He pinched me and pulled my hair with **three** different hands at once.

'Agh!' I yelled, letting go of him.

'Ha ha!' he laughed, and turned to run away, but Grandad seized him by his feet and pulled the **sock** off his head. The Klepto shrieked and hissed at him.

CHAPTER 4

The Klepto Code

'We're not going to hurt you,'
Grandad said to the Klepto, as he held
him up. 'We just want to know **what**
you are. And what you're doing down
the back of my sofa.'

'You don't have to shout! I'm a
Klepto. I've got **very, very** good
hearing.'

The skinny creature covered his ears. 'My name's Nickit, and that was my sister, Pinch. That's all I have to tell you. Them's the **Rules**.'

'What rules?' I asked.

'Don't you know anything? It's the **The Klepto Code**,' Nickit snorted.

Rule 1: Steal Everything.

Rule 2: Don't Get Caught.

Rule 3: Don't Talk to Strangers.

Rule 4: Steal Everything.

'You said that last one twice,' I said to him.

'We like that one,' he snapped.

'You can't just go round stealing things,' Grandad growled at him.

'Of course we can,' Nickit sighed. 'We do it all the time. It's easy! You sleep all day – especially when we take your alarm clock! We have to keep robbing them, and we **HATE** alarm clocks.'

Suddenly Pinch, Nickit's sister, appeared out of nowhere and pointed the nozzle of a **vacuum cleaner** at us.

'So that's where my hoover got to,' Grandad said.

Pinch aimed the nozzle at us and flicked the switch. Hundreds of hard, slightly hairy **sweets** blasted out at us. It was like being hit by stones.

'Aagh!' Grandad cried. 'They've made a **gun** out of it! Run, Lenny!'

We started to run, but more and more of the sweets stuck to our clothes and our skin. In seconds, we were so covered by sweets, we could hardly move.

44

Grandad tripped, and rolled down a slope, and I tumbled down after him. We crashed into a stack of shelves holding dozens of **alarm clocks**, and they toppled over on top of us.

CHAPTER 5

Old Mother Klepto

'What's all that noise?' a **nasty** voice
hissed.

We dragged ourselves out from
under the clocks, and scraped the
tacky sweets away. At first, we
couldn't see where the **voice** was
coming from. Then we looked up.

Hanging from a spring above us, was a **huge** creature with loads of arms and legs sticking out of a small, wrinkled body. Evil, squinty eyes stared down at us.

'We stole them, Mammy!' Nickit called from behind us. 'We stole them for you!'

'For me?' the Kleptoes' mother cackled. 'Thank you, children! You always know just what to steal for your dear old mother. What lovely **pets** they'll make!'

'You won't make pets of us!'
Grandad shouted, picking something
off the ground.

The creature grabbed him by his
ankle, and hoisted him into the air.

'Don't raise your voice with me,
lovey,' she snapped. 'Old Mother
Klepto has such sensitive ears. You
and this little one will make **darling**
pets.'

She snatched me up too, and turned towards an enormous **fish tank** in the corner of the room. She was going to trap us inside!

'Don't you **dare**!' she hissed.

But Grandad set the alarm and it went off. The evil old monster dropped us, and **cowered** away, covering her ears. We had just enough time to get to our feet, before she bared her teeth and came after us again.

CHAPTER 6

The Old Sofa Goes for Good

We both grabbed some clocks and
started running. The **Kleptoes**
followed us, but we kept setting clocks
and throwing them behind us.

The alarms drove the Kleptoes
mad, and they had to stop and **stamp**
on each one.

We made it to where we had come
in. I threw down our last clock and we
started climbing. As we clambered
out, we heard the ringing stop behind
us, and then the **snarling** sound of
Old Mother Klepto coming after us.

'Quick, Lenny!' Grandad called, as he picked up his new clock to fend them off. 'Turn on the **stereo**! And turn the volume right up!'

I did like he said, and it worked. The noise kept the Kleptoes inside the sofa. Grandad called some men with a van and we sent that sofa to the dump. We thought the Kleptoes would be **happy** there.

Grandad bought a brand new sofa, and we checked the back of it **really carefully** before it was delivered. Things still go missing sometimes, but as Grandad says; you can't blame the sofa for everything.